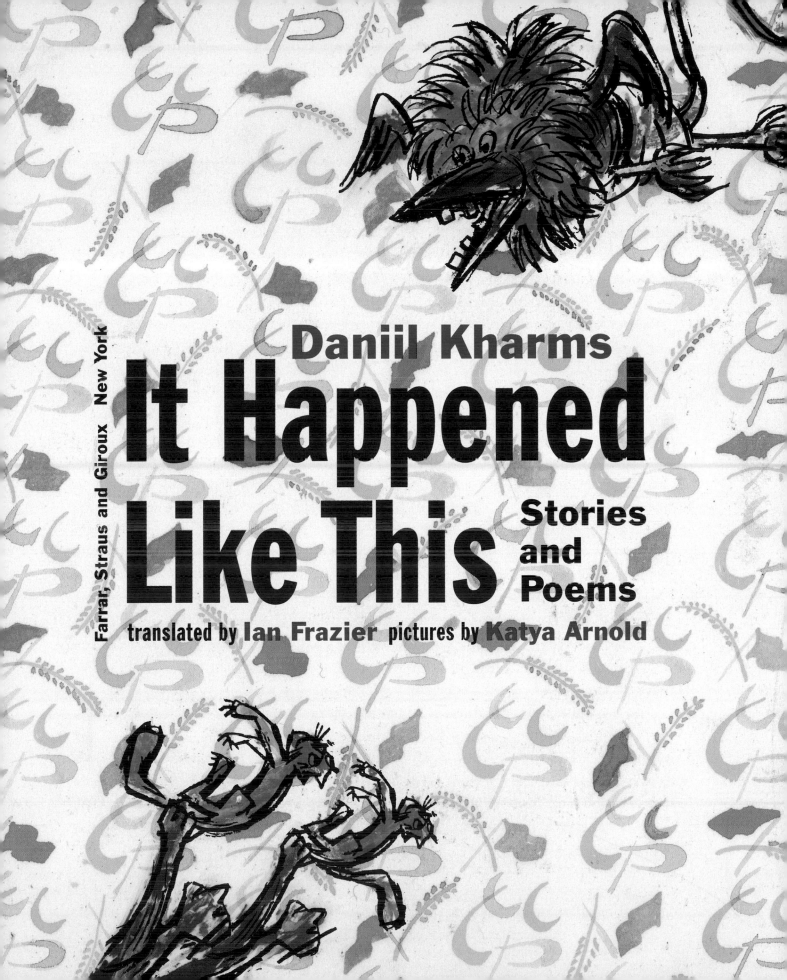

Daniil Kharms

It Happened Like This

Farrar, Straus and Giroux   New York

Stories and Poems

translated by **Ian Frazier**   pictures by **Katya Arnold**

Introduction

Daniil Kharms was a funny writer and a brave man. The first letter of his last name, in Russian, is **X**, which makes a sound down in the throat like the beginning of a cough. It is sort of hard to say in English. He made up that name for himself; his real name was Daniil (like Daniel) Ivanovich Yuvachov. He was born almost a hundred years ago and he died over fifty years ago. He lived in Russia, which was a scary and dangerous place, especially for writers, at that time. When Daniil was born, in the city of St. Petersburg, people were trying to get rid of the emperor, called the tsar. The tsar imprisoned some of them, including Daniil's father, who was sent to Siberia for a while. Daniil's father was a writer and a scientist, and he liked to write wild, strange stories and read them to his son. Daniil grew up in St. Petersburg and went to school there. By the time he was a teenager the tsar was dead, killed by the Communists, who had set up their own government. Eventually the Communists imprisoned and killed more people than the tsar ever had.

Daniil studied different subjects in college, but decided he wanted to be a poet. He started reading his poems in public, and he got together with other writers who liked the same kinds of writing that he did. Much of this writing is what is called absurd, which means that it didn't always make sense. Daniil also did funny things just for the heck of it. For example, although he was not a rich person, he sometimes went around dressed like one, to tease the Communists, who didn't like rich people. They didn't like him or his friends much, either, and before long he couldn't get his plays produced or his poems published. That's when he started writing for children's magazines. Although he was often gloomy and said he didn't like anybody, he wrote lighthearted, original, amazing children's stories and poems for many years. They became favorites among Russian children, and still are today.

As the Communist government began to imprison more and more people, friends of Daniil began to disappear. He feared he would disappear soon, too, and he was right. One morning the police came and took him from his apartment without even giving him time to change from his bedroom slippers into his shoes. He never came home again; later his wife learned that he had died. In this book are just a few of his stories and poems, works of the imagination which effortlessly overcome the sadness of his life.

Contents

A Mysterious Case 4

Have You Been to the Zoo? 8

The Carpenter Kushakoff 12

The Four-Legged Crow 18

Balloons Are Flying 20

What Comes First? 24

The Writing Guy 28

Optical Illusion 32

Let's Write a Story 36

A Man Left His House 46

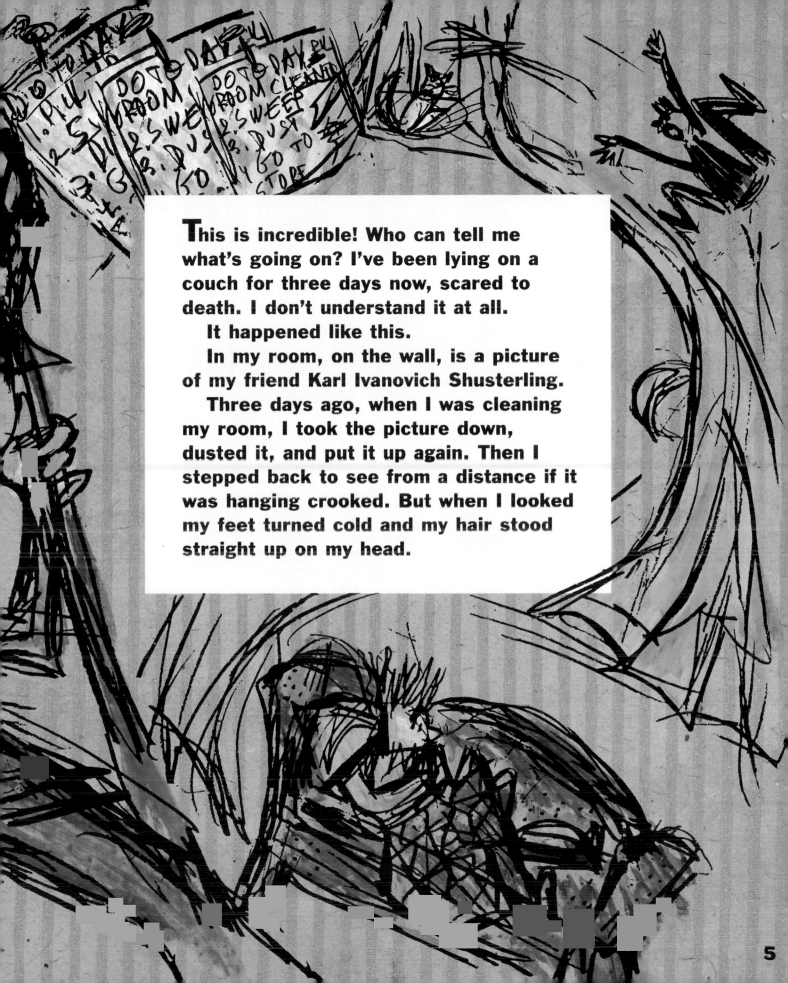

This is incredible! Who can tell me what's going on? I've been lying on a couch for three days now, scared to death. I don't understand it at all.

It happened like this.

In my room, on the wall, is a picture of my friend Karl Ivanovich Shusterling.

Three days ago, when I was cleaning my room, I took the picture down, dusted it, and put it up again. Then I stepped back to see from a distance if it was hanging crooked. But when I looked my feet turned cold and my hair stood straight up on my head.

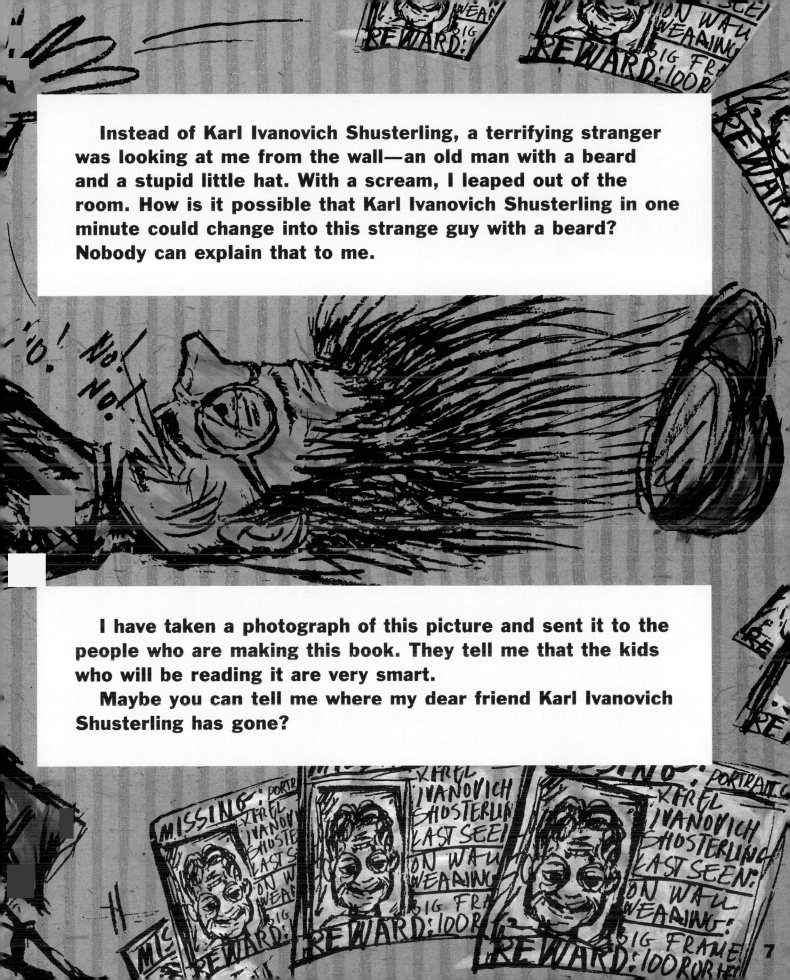

Instead of Karl Ivanovich Shusterling, a terrifying stranger was looking at me from the wall—an old man with a beard and a stupid little hat. With a scream, I leaped out of the room. How is it possible that Karl Ivanovich Shusterling in one minute could change into this strange guy with a beard? Nobody can explain that to me.

I have taken a photograph of this picture and sent it to the people who are making this book. They tell me that the kids who will be reading it are very smart.

Maybe you can tell me where my dear friend Karl Ivanovich Shusterling has gone?

"Have you been to the zoo?"
"Yes, I've been there."
"Have you seen the lion?"
"With the trunk?"
"No, that's an elephant. A lion isn't like that."
"Oh, you mean with the two humps."
"No, not like that! With a mane!"
"Yes, yes, with a mane, and a beak."
"What do you mean, beak? With *teeth*, big teeth."
"Okay, yes, with teeth and with wings."
"No. That's not a lion."
"What is it, then?"
"That I don't know. A lion is yellow."
"Okay, yes—yellow, almost a gray."
"No, more like almost reddish."

"Yes, yes, yes—with a tail."

"Yes, with a tail and claws."

"Right! With claws, and about as big as an inkwell."

"What kind of lion would that be? That's more likely a mouse."

"Come on! A mouse doesn't have wings."

"This had wings?"

"Definitely!"

"Then it has to be a bird."

"Right, right—a bird. I agree."

"But I was talking about a lion."

"I was, too—a lion bird."

"Really, though. A lion is a bird?"

"In my opinion, it is a bird. And it always chirps like this: *Tirlee, tirlee, tweet-tweet-tweet.*"

"Wait a minute. Is it gray and yellow?"

"Yes. Gray and yellow."

"With a little round head?"

"Yes, a little round head."

"And it flies?"

"It flies."

"Let me tell you: that's a finch."

"Of course! A finch!"

"But I was asking about a lion."

"No, I haven't seen a lion."

KUSHAK = BELT
(IN RUSSIAN)

KUSHAKOFF =
McBELT

The Carpenter Kushakoff

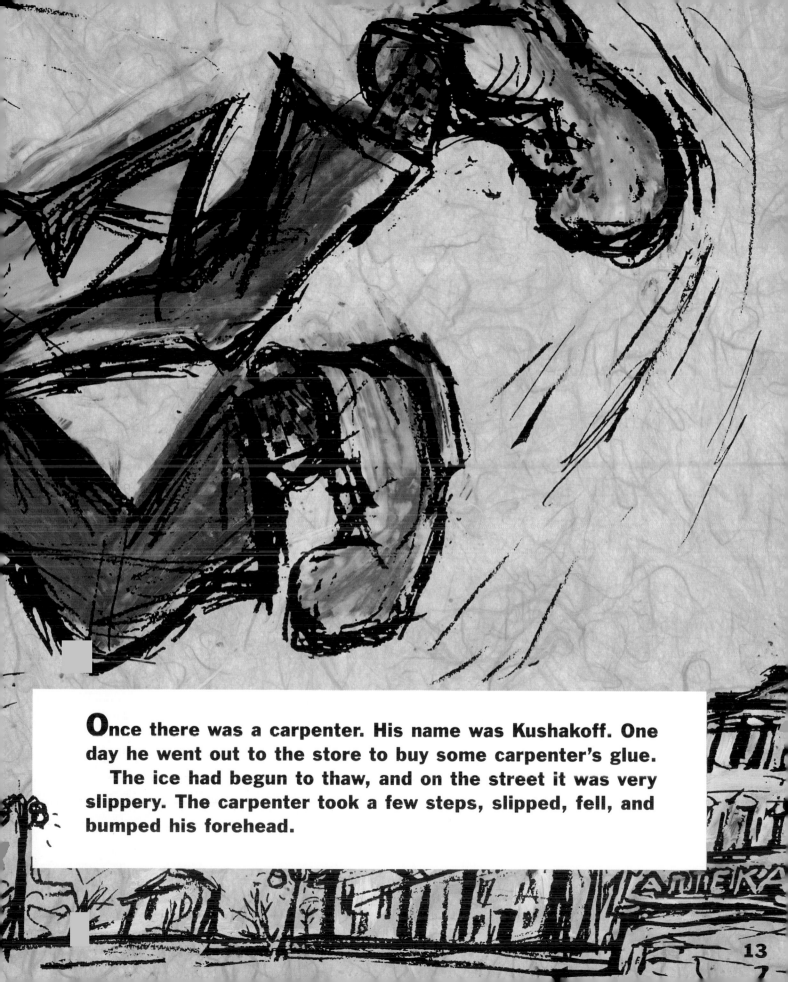

Once there was a carpenter. His name was Kushakoff. One day he went out to the store to buy some carpenter's glue.

The ice had begun to thaw, and on the street it was very slippery. The carpenter took a few steps, slipped, fell, and bumped his forehead.

"Ouch!" said the carpenter. He got up, went to the drugstore, bought a bandage, and stuck it on his forehead.

But when he went out on the street and tried to take a few steps, he slipped again, fell, and bumped his nose. "Ufff!" said the carpenter, and he went back to the drugstore, bought a bandage, and stuck the bandage on his nose.

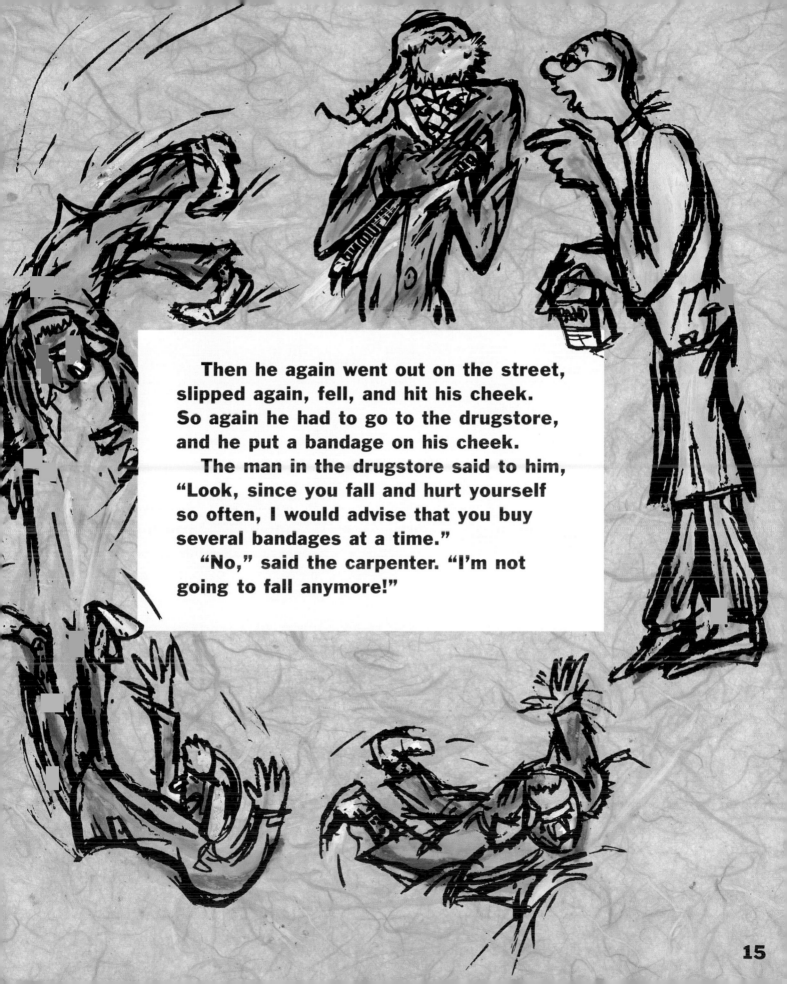

Then he again went out on the street,
slipped again, fell, and hit his cheek.
So again he had to go to the drugstore,
and he put a bandage on his cheek.

The man in the drugstore said to him,
"Look, since you fall and hurt yourself
so often, I would advise that you buy
several bandages at a time."

"No," said the carpenter. "I'm not
going to fall anymore!"

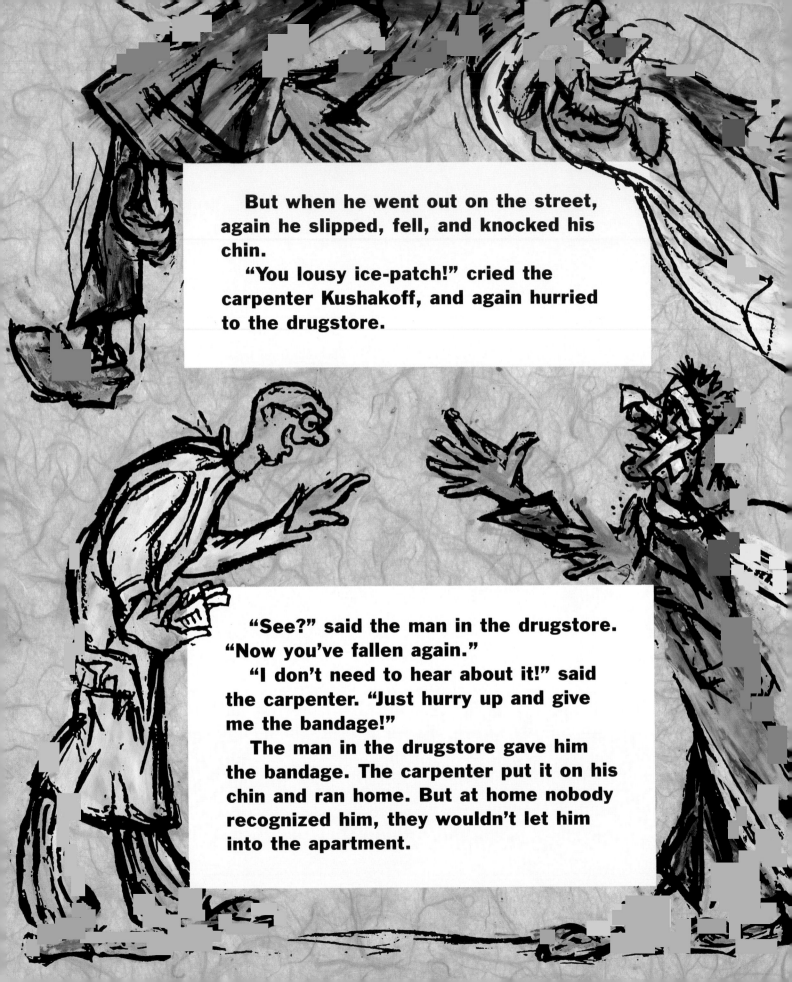

But when he went out on the street, again he slipped, fell, and knocked his chin.

"You lousy ice-patch!" cried the carpenter Kushakoff, and again hurried to the drugstore.

"See?" said the man in the drugstore. "Now you've fallen again."

"I don't need to hear about it!" said the carpenter. "Just hurry up and give me the bandage!"

The man in the drugstore gave him the bandage. The carpenter put it on his chin and ran home. But at home nobody recognized him, they wouldn't let him into the apartment.

"I'm the carpenter Kushakoff!" cried the carpenter.

"Tell us another one!" they answered from inside the apartment, sliding the chain into the lock.

The carpenter Kushakoff stood for a while on the stairs, spat, and went out on the street.

Once upon a time there was a crow with four legs. To tell the truth, he actually had five legs, but there's no reason to mention that.

One day the four-legged crow bought himself some coffee, and he thought, "Well, now I've bought myself some coffee, but what do I do with it?"

At that moment, by a stroke of bad luck, a fox came running by.

The Four-Legged Crow

He saw the crow and cried out to him, "Hey, you ol' crow!"

The crow yelled back at the fox, "You're an old crow yourself!"

The fox yelled back at the crow, "And you, crow, are a real pig!"

At this the crow was so offended he spilled his coffee. The fox ran off. The crow got down on the ground and walked away on his four, or actually five, legs to his horrible house.

In the sky, balloons are flying;
They fly up there, they fly;
In the sky, balloons are flying,
Shining and rustling as they go by.

In the sky, balloons are flying;
The people wave at them, goodbye;
In the sky, balloons are flying;
The people wave at them, goodbye.

In the sky, balloons are flying;
The people wave with hats, goodbye;
In the sky, balloons are flying;
The people wave with canes, goodbye.

In the sky, balloons are flying;
The people wave with rolls, goodbye;
In the sky, balloons are flying;
The people wave with cats, goodbye.

In the sky, balloons are flying;
The people wave with chairs, goodbye;
In the sky, balloons are flying;
The people wave with lamps, goodbye.

In the sky, balloons are flying;
The people stay to watch them fly.
In the sky, balloons are flying,
Shining and rustling as they go by.
And the people, too, make a rustling sigh.

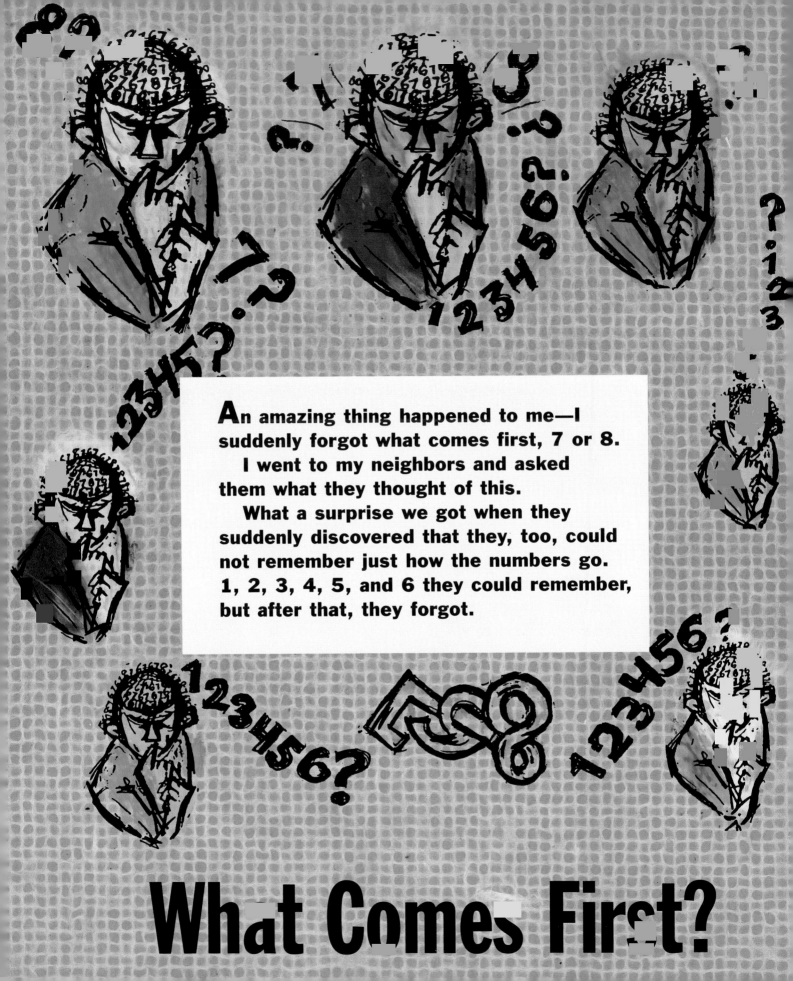

An amazing thing happened to me—I suddenly forgot what comes first, 7 or 8.
I went to my neighbors and asked them what they thought of this.
What a surprise we got when they suddenly discovered that they, too, could not remember just how the numbers go. 1, 2, 3, 4, 5, and 6 they could remember, but after that, they forgot.

What Comes First?

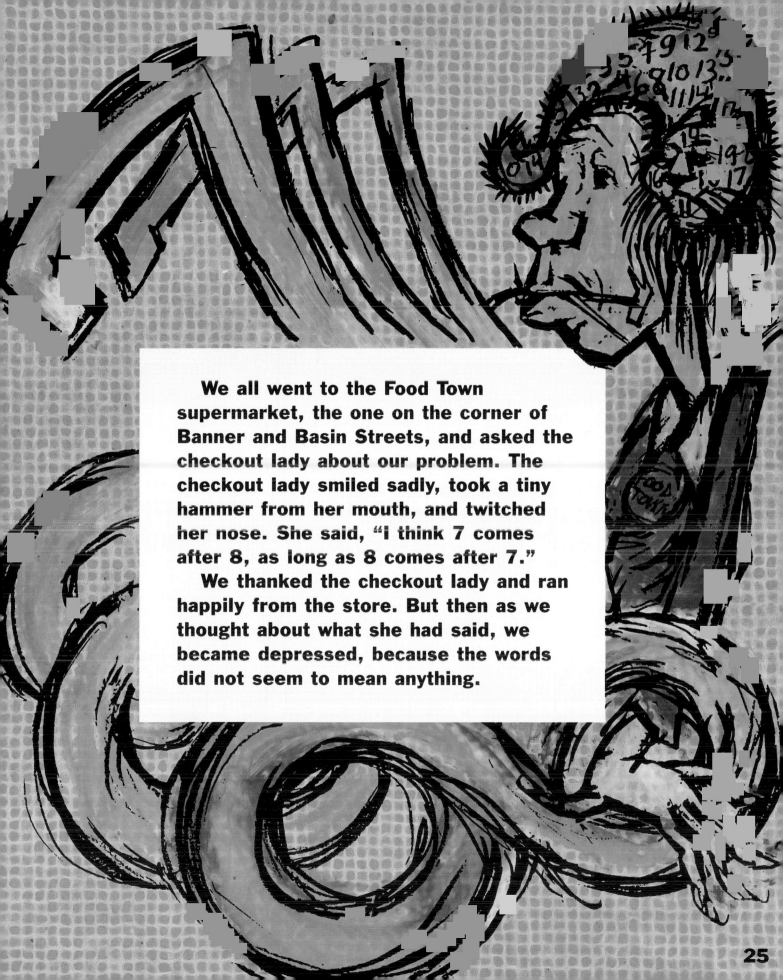

We all went to the Food Town supermarket, the one on the corner of Banner and Basin Streets, and asked the checkout lady about our problem. The checkout lady smiled sadly, took a tiny hammer from her mouth, and twitched her nose. She said, "I think 7 comes after 8, as long as 8 comes after 7."

We thanked the checkout lady and ran happily from the store. But then as we thought about what she had said, we became depressed, because the words did not seem to mean anything.

What could we do? We went to the park and started to count the trees. But when we got to the sixth tree, we stopped and began to argue; some of us thought that 7 was next, and others thought 8 was next.

We argued for a very long time, but
then by chance a little kid fell off a park
bench and broke both jaws. So we forgot
what we were arguing about.
Then we all went home.

OUCH!

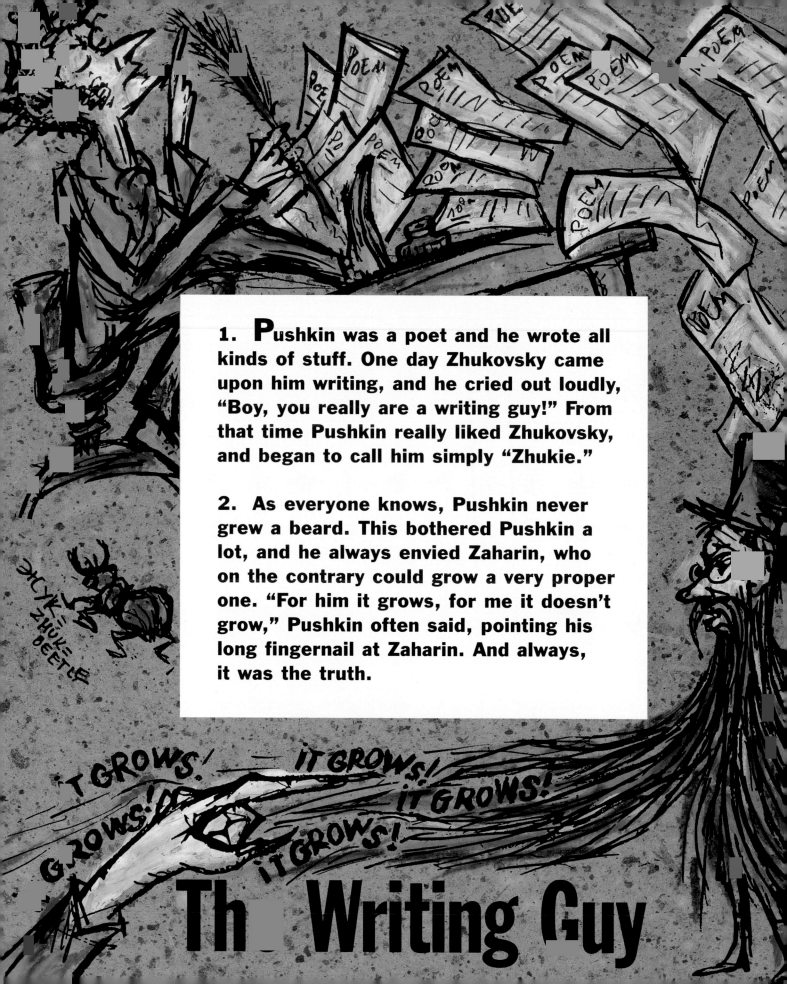

1. **P**ushkin was a poet and he wrote all kinds of stuff. One day Zhukovsky came upon him writing, and he cried out loudly, "Boy, you really are a writing guy!" From that time Pushkin really liked Zhukovsky, and began to call him simply "Zhukie."

2. As everyone knows, Pushkin never grew a beard. This bothered Pushkin a lot, and he always envied Zaharin, who on the contrary could grow a very proper one. "For him it grows, for me it doesn't grow," Pushkin often said, pointing his long fingernail at Zaharin. And always, it was the truth.

Th Writing Guy

3. One day Petrushevsky's watch broke, and he called Pushkin. Pushkin came over, looked at Petrushevsky's watch, and put it back on the chair. "What do you say, brother Pushkin?" Petrushevsky asked. "No go," said Pushkin.

4. When Pushkin broke his leg, he had to go around on wheels. His friends liked to tease Pushkin and grab him by the wheels. This made Pushkin angry, and he wrote nasty poems about them. He called these poems "erpigrams."

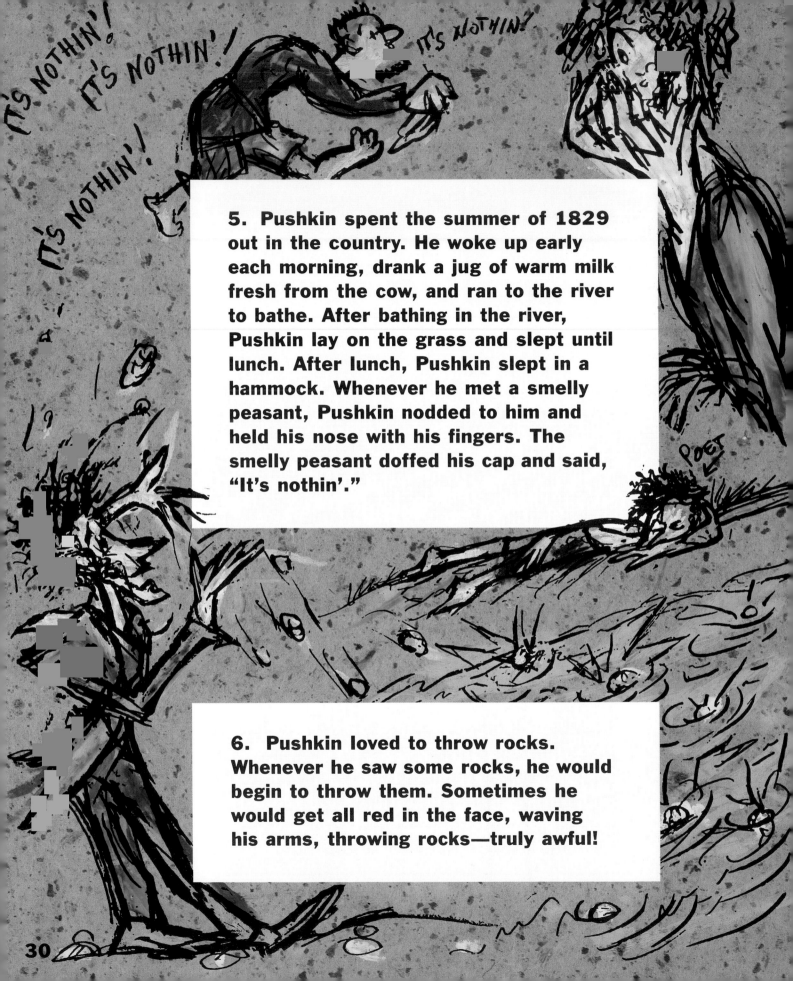

5. Pushkin spent the summer of 1829 out in the country. He woke up early each morning, drank a jug of warm milk fresh from the cow, and ran to the river to bathe. After bathing in the river, Pushkin lay on the grass and slept until lunch. After lunch, Pushkin slept in a hammock. Whenever he met a smelly peasant, Pushkin nodded to him and held his nose with his fingers. The smelly peasant doffed his cap and said, "It's nothin'."

6. Pushkin loved to throw rocks. Whenever he saw some rocks, he would begin to throw them. Sometimes he would get all red in the face, waving his arms, throwing rocks—truly awful!

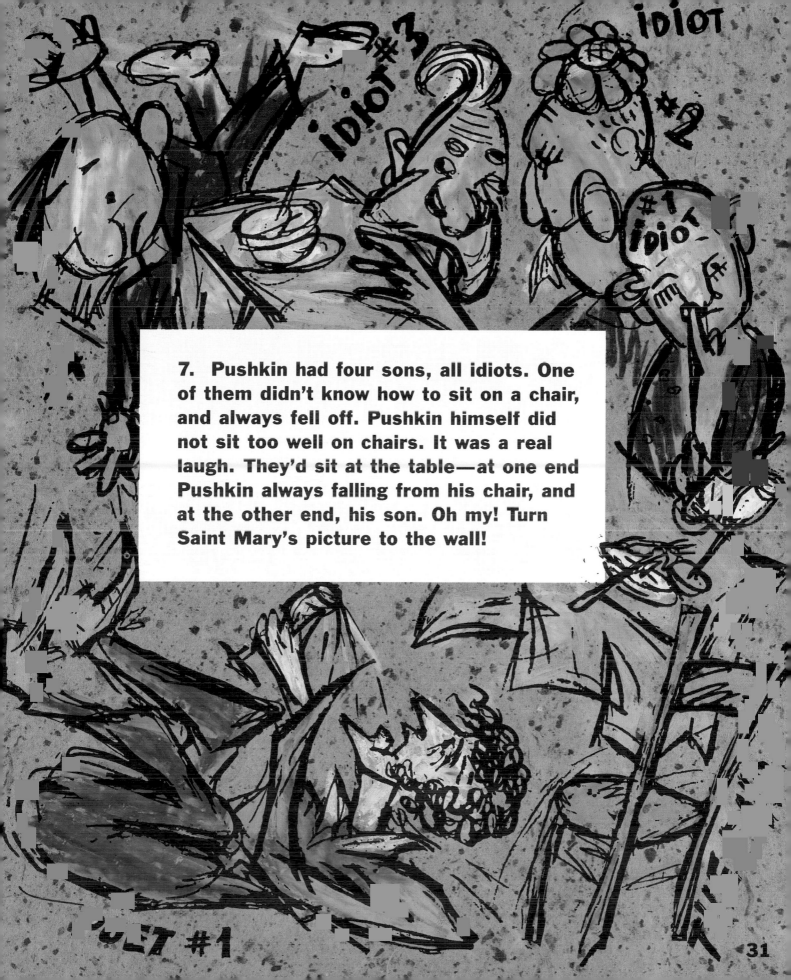

7. Pushkin had four sons, all idiots. One of them didn't know how to sit on a chair, and always fell off. Pushkin himself did not sit too well on chairs. It was a real laugh. They'd sit at the table—at one end Pushkin always falling from his chair, and at the other end, his son. Oh my! Turn Saint Mary's picture to the wall!

Optical Illusion

Simon Simonson, putting on his glasses, looks in a tree and sees a man sitting in the tree shaking his fist at him.

Simon Simonson, taking off his glasses, looks in the tree and sees that no one is sitting there.

Simon Simonson, putting on his glasses, looks in the tree and again sees a man sitting in the tree and shaking his fist at him.

Simon Simonson, taking off his glasses, again sees that no one is sitting in the tree.

Simon Simonson, again putting on his glasses, looks in the tree and again sees that a man is sitting there shaking his fist at him.

Simon Simonson does not want to believe he sees this, so he calls it an optical illusion.

"Here," said Boris, putting a notebook on the table, "let's write a story."

"Okay," said Sonya as she sat down at a chair.

Boris took a pencil and began to write: "Once upon a time there was a king . . ."

Then Boris stopped and thought, looking up toward the ceiling. Sonya glanced at the notebook and read what Boris had written.

"There already is a story like that," Sonya said.

"How do you know?" asked Boris.

"I know because I read it," Sonya said.

"Well, what is the story about, then?" Boris asked.

LEMON = APPLES

(WHEN PUT IN TEA)

TEA AND APPLE

Let's Write a Story

"Well, it's about how a king was having some tea with apples in it, and suddenly he began to choke, and the queen began to pound him on the back to get the piece of apple to come out. But the king thought the queen was fighting with him, so he hit her over the head with his cup. Then the queen got mad and hit the king with a plate. Then the king hit the queen with a bowl. Then the queen hit the king with a chair.

CHAIR

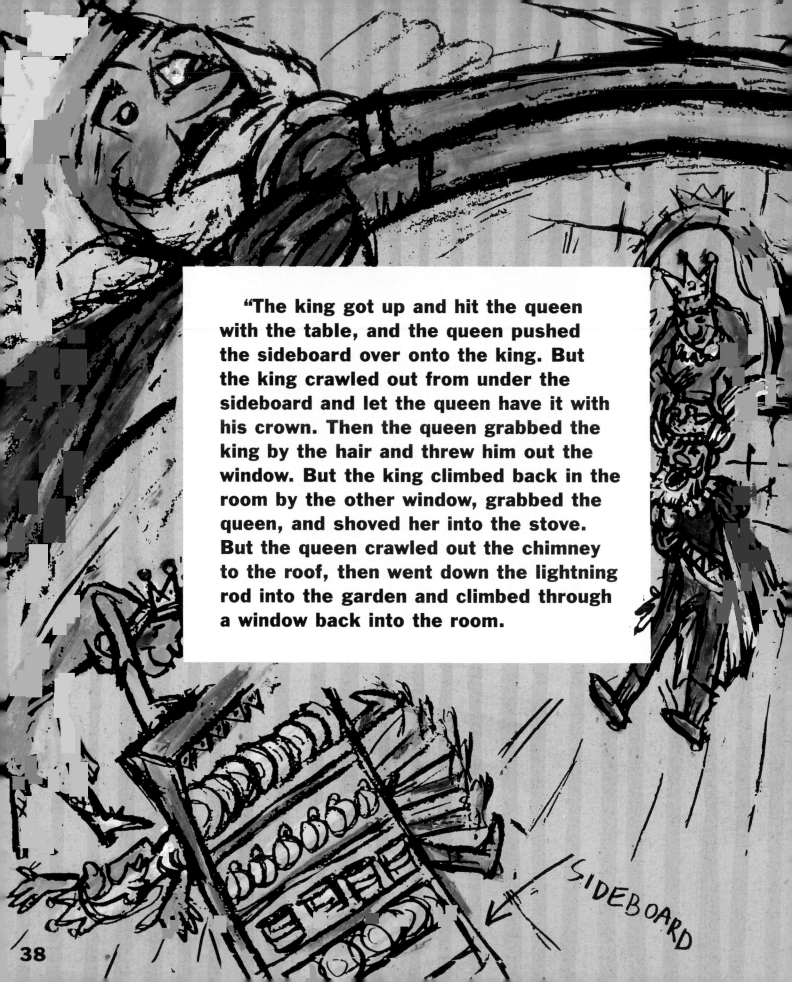

"The king got up and hit the queen
with the table, and the queen pushed
the sideboard over onto the king. But
the king crawled out from under the
sideboard and let the queen have it with
his crown. Then the queen grabbed the
king by the hair and threw him out the
window. But the king climbed back in the
room by the other window, grabbed the
queen, and shoved her into the stove.
But the queen crawled out the chimney
to the roof, then went down the lightning
rod into the garden and climbed through
a window back into the room.

SIDEBOARD

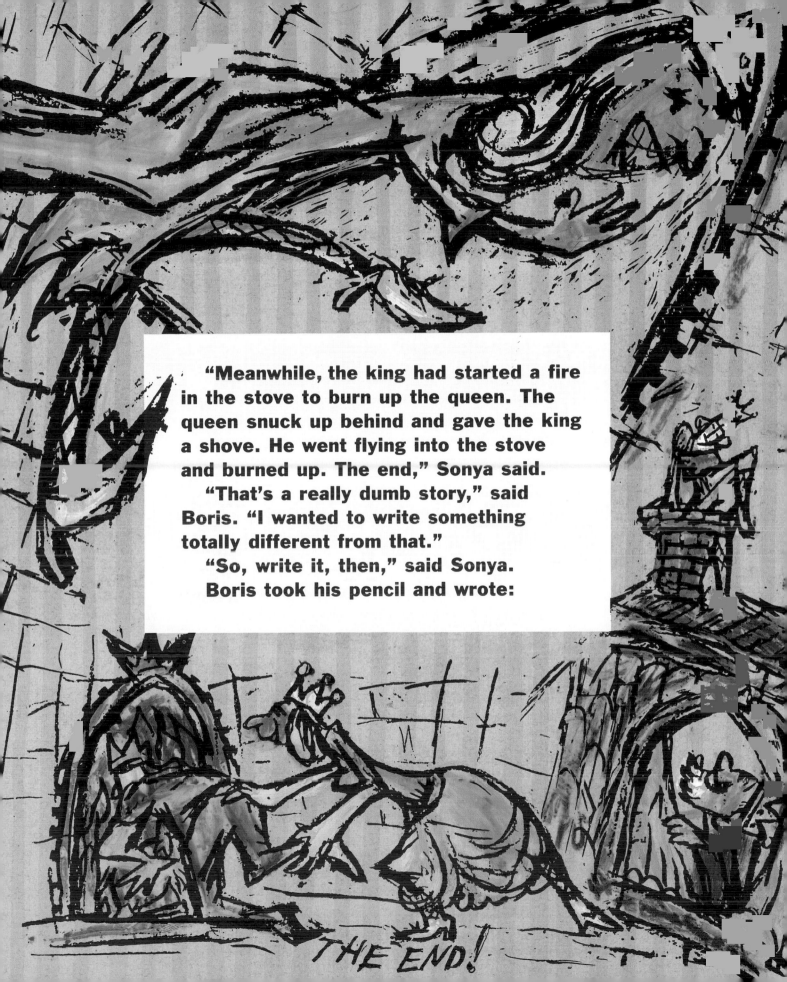

"Meanwhile, the king had started a fire in the stove to burn up the queen. The queen snuck up behind and gave the king a shove. He went flying into the stove and burned up. The end," Sonya said.

"That's a really dumb story," said Boris. "I wanted to write something totally different from that."

"So, write it, then," said Sonya.

Boris took his pencil and wrote:

THE END!

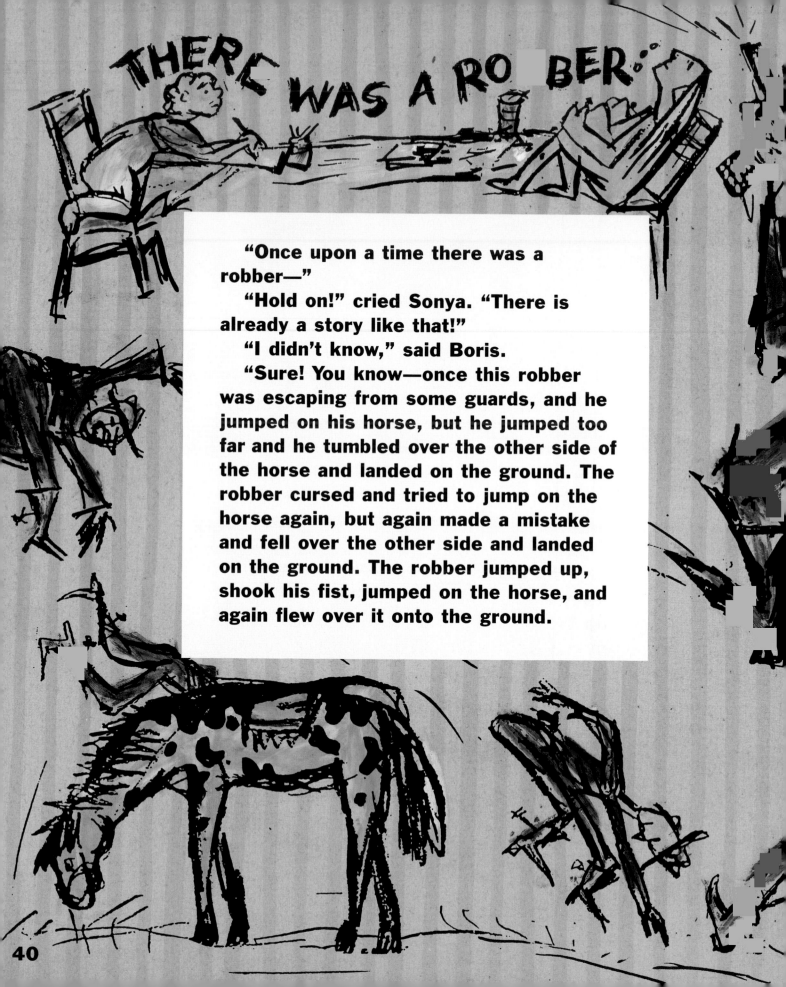

"Once upon a time there was a robber—"

"Hold on!" cried Sonya. "There is already a story like that!"

"I didn't know," said Boris.

"Sure! You know—once this robber was escaping from some guards, and he jumped on his horse, but he jumped too far and he tumbled over the other side of the horse and landed on the ground. The robber cursed and tried to jump on the horse again, but again made a mistake and fell over the other side and landed on the ground. The robber jumped up, shook his fist, jumped on the horse, and again flew over it onto the ground.

"Then the robber pulled a gun from his belt and shot into the air, and again jumped on the horse, but so hard that again he went way over and crashed down on the ground.

"Then the robber yanked his hat from his head, stamped on it with his feet, and again jumped on the horse, and again fell over it, crashed on the ground, and broke his leg. The horse moved away a little bit. The limping robber went up to the horse and hit it between the eyes with his fist. The horse ran away. Meanwhile, the guards came riding up. They caught the robber and took him to prison."

THE END!

"Well, so I won't write about a robber," said Boris.

"About what, then?" asked Sonya.

"I'll write a story about a blacksmith," Boris said.

Boris wrote: "Once upon a time there was a blacksmith—"

"There's a story like that, too!" cried Sonya.

"Really?" said Boris, putting down his pencil.

"Really," said Sonya.

BLACKSMITH MAKES HORSESHOES, SWORDS...

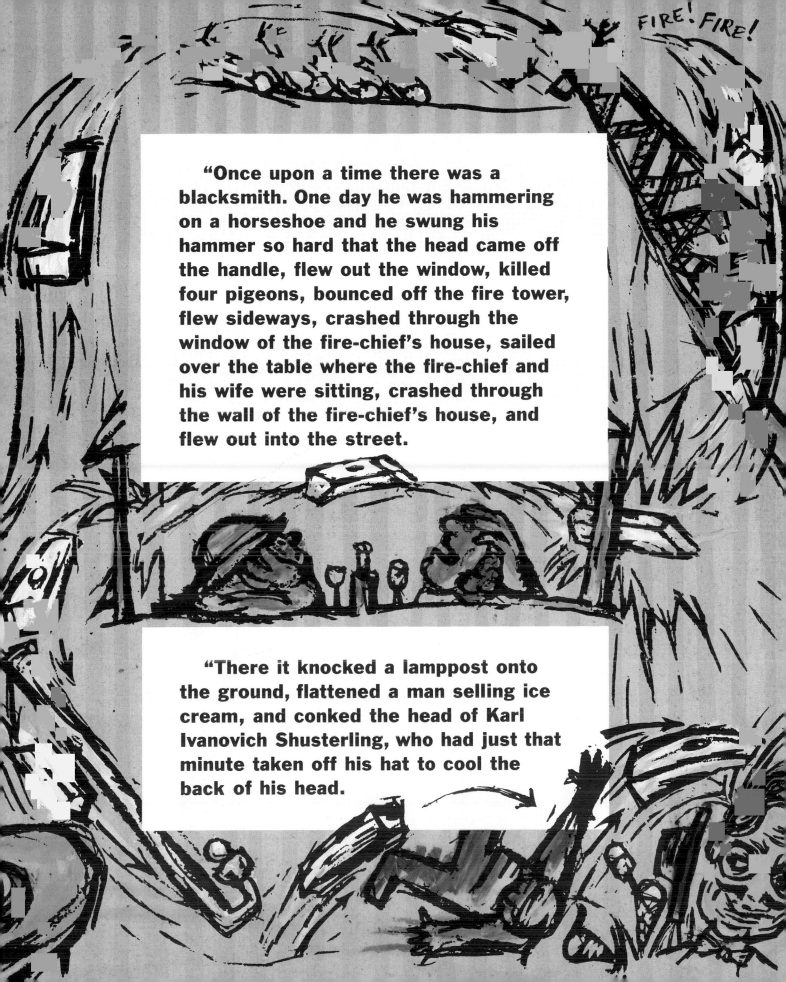

"Once upon a time there was a blacksmith. One day he was hammering on a horseshoe and he swung his hammer so hard that the head came off the handle, flew out the window, killed four pigeons, bounced off the fire tower, flew sideways, crashed through the window of the fire-chief's house, sailed over the table where the fire-chief and his wife were sitting, crashed through the wall of the fire-chief's house, and flew out into the street.

"There it knocked a lamppost onto the ground, flattened a man selling ice cream, and conked the head of Karl Ivanovich Shusterling, who had just that minute taken off his hat to cool the back of his head.

"Bouncing off Karl Ivanovich Shusterling's head, the hammer flew back the other way, again knocked the ice-cream man off his feet, knocked down two cats who were fighting on the roof, tipped over a cow, killed four sparrows, and flew into the blacksmith shop back onto the handle, which the blacksmith was still holding in his right hand. All this happened so fast that the blacksmith didn't notice a thing and just went on hammering at his horseshoe."

"All right, if there's already a story about a blacksmith, then I'll write a story about myself," said Boris, and he wrote: "Once upon a time there was a boy named Boris—"

"There's also a story about Boris," said Sonya. "Once upon a time there was a boy named Boris, and one day he—"

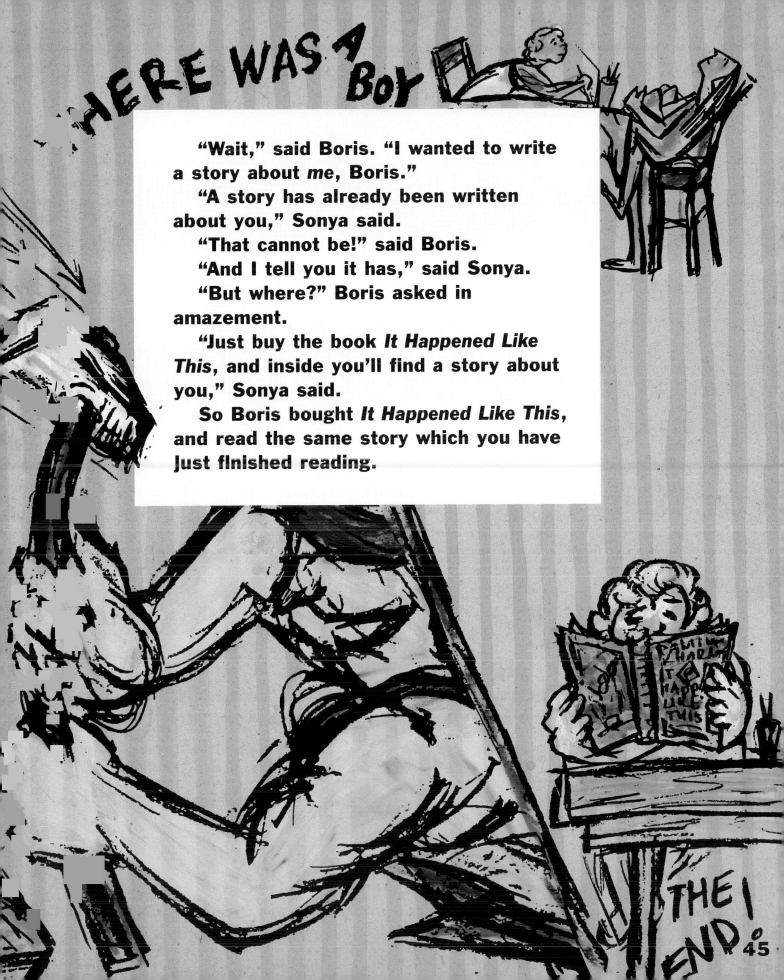

"Wait," said Boris. "I wanted to write a story about *me*, Boris."

"A story has already been written about you," Sonya said.

"That cannot be!" said Boris.

"And I tell you it has," said Sonya.

"But where?" Boris asked in amazement.

"Just buy the book *It Happened Like This*, and inside you'll find a story about you," Sonya said.

So Boris bought *It Happened Like This*, and read the same story which you have just finished reading.

THE END

A man left his house
With a club and a sack
And on a long journey
And on a long journey
He set off on foot.

He walked always straight ahead
And always looked ahead.
He didn't sleep, he didn't drink,
He didn't drink, he didn't sleep,
He didn't sleep or drink or eat.

A Man Left His Hous

And then one day at dawn
He went into a dark forest.
And from that time,
And from that time,
And from that time, he disappeared.

But if by some chance
You should happen to meet him,
Then quickly
Quickly
Quickly come and tell us.

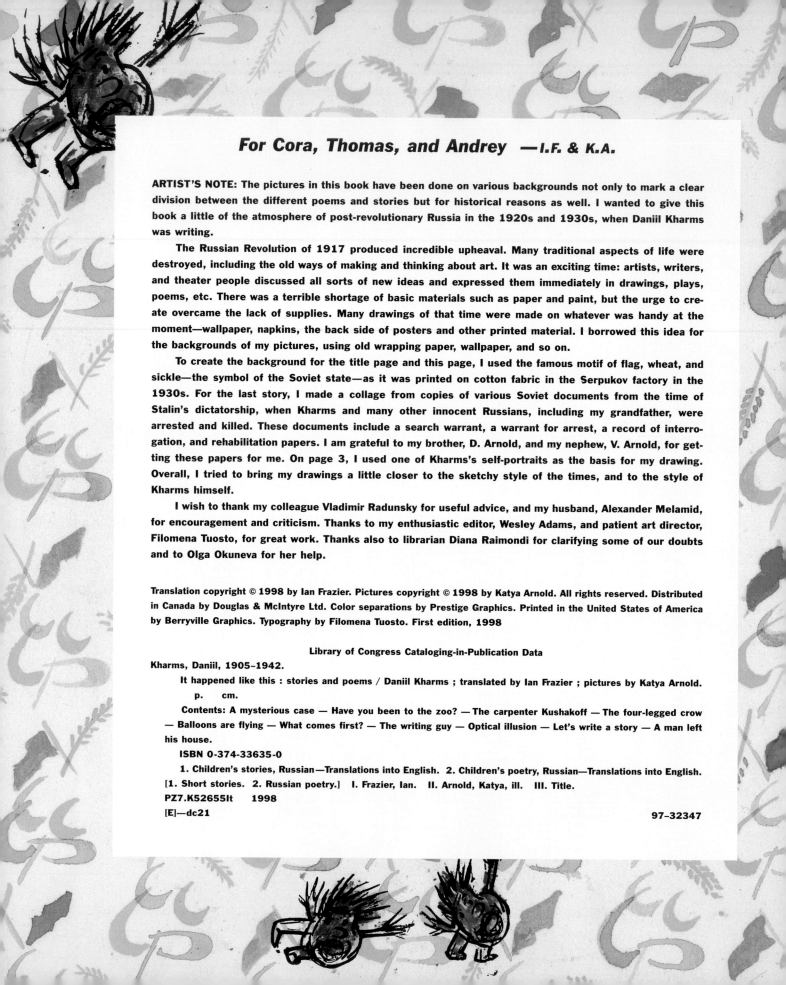

For Cora, Thomas, and Andrey —I.F. & K.A.

ARTIST'S NOTE: The pictures in this book have been done on various backgrounds not only to mark a clear division between the different poems and stories but for historical reasons as well. I wanted to give this book a little of the atmosphere of post-revolutionary Russia in the 1920s and 1930s, when Daniil Kharms was writing.

The Russian Revolution of 1917 produced incredible upheaval. Many traditional aspects of life were destroyed, including the old ways of making and thinking about art. It was an exciting time: artists, writers, and theater people discussed all sorts of new ideas and expressed them immediately in drawings, plays, poems, etc. There was a terrible shortage of basic materials such as paper and paint, but the urge to create overcame the lack of supplies. Many drawings of that time were made on whatever was handy at the moment—wallpaper, napkins, the back side of posters and other printed material. I borrowed this idea for the backgrounds of my pictures, using old wrapping paper, wallpaper, and so on.

To create the background for the title page and this page, I used the famous motif of flag, wheat, and sickle—the symbol of the Soviet state—as it was printed on cotton fabric in the Serpukov factory in the 1930s. For the last story, I made a collage from copies of various Soviet documents from the time of Stalin's dictatorship, when Kharms and many other innocent Russians, including my grandfather, were arrested and killed. These documents include a search warrant, a warrant for arrest, a record of interrogation, and rehabilitation papers. I am grateful to my brother, D. Arnold, and my nephew, V. Arnold, for getting these papers for me. On page 3, I used one of Kharms's self-portraits as the basis for my drawing. Overall, I tried to bring my drawings a little closer to the sketchy style of the times, and to the style of Kharms himself.

I wish to thank my colleague Vladimir Radunsky for useful advice, and my husband, Alexander Melamid, for encouragement and criticism. Thanks to my enthusiastic editor, Wesley Adams, and patient art director, Filomena Tuosto, for great work. Thanks also to librarian Diana Raimondi for clarifying some of our doubts and to Olga Okuneva for her help.

Translation copyright © 1998 by Ian Frazier. Pictures copyright © 1998 by Katya Arnold. All rights reserved. Distributed in Canada by Douglas & McIntyre Ltd. Color separations by Prestige Graphics. Printed in the United States of America by Berryville Graphics. Typography by Filomena Tuosto. First edition, 1998

Library of Congress Cataloging-in-Publication Data

Kharms, Daniil, 1905–1942.
    It happened like this : stories and poems / Daniil Kharms ; translated by Ian Frazier ; pictures by Katya Arnold.
       p.   cm.
    Contents: A mysterious case — Have you been to the zoo? — The carpenter Kushakoff — The four-legged crow — Balloons are flying — What comes first? — The writing guy — Optical illusion — Let's write a story — A man left his house.
    ISBN 0-374-33635-0
    1. Children's stories, Russian—Translations into English. 2. Children's poetry, Russian—Translations into English.
[1. Short stories. 2. Russian poetry.] I. Frazier, Ian. II. Arnold, Katya, ill. III. Title.
PZ7.K52655It   1998
[E]—dc21
                                       97-32347